THREE WISHES

For A.M.B.

PUFFIN BOOKS
Published by the Penguin Group
Penguin Books USA Inc., 375 Hudson Street, New York, New York 10014, U.S.A.
Penguin Books Ltd, 27 Wrights Lane, London W8 5TZ, England
Penguin Books Australia Ltd, Ringwood, Victoria, Australia
Penguin Books Canada Ltd, 10 Alcorn Avenue, Toronto, Ontario, Canada M4V 3B2
Penguin Books (N.Z.) Ltd, 182-190 Wairau Road, Auckland 10, New Zealand
Penguin Books Ltd, Registered Offices: Harmondsworth, Middlesex, England

First published in the United States of America by Viking Penguin,
a division of Penguin Books USA Inc., 1993
Published simultaneously in a Puffin Books edition
Published in a Puffin Easy-to-Read edition, 1996

3 5 7 9 10 8 6 4

Text copyright © Harriet Ziefert, 1993
Illustrations copyright © David Jacobson, 1993
All rights reserved

THE LIBRARY OF CONGRESS HAS CATALOGED THE VIKING EDITION
UNDER CATALOG CARD NUMBER 92-80383
THE LIBRARY OF CONGRESS HAS CATALOGED THE PREVIOUS PUFFIN EDITION
UNDER CATALOG CARD NUMBER 92-80245

Puffin® and Easy-to-Read® are registered trademarks of Penguin Books USA Inc.

Puffin Easy-to-Read ISBN 0-14-038323-9
Printed in the United States of America

Reading Level 2.2

THREE WISHES

Harriet Ziefert
Pictures by David Jacobson

PUFFIN BOOKS

Chapter One

Morning Wish

I want to fish
in the pond
outside.

I want to put
my fishing line
in the water.

I want to pull…

and pull…

and pull.

And, before I'm done,
I want to pull out
two hundred…

and twenty-two fishes!

I want to be
boss of the kitchen…

and eat just how I want.

I'll sit at the head
of the table.

I'll begin with raisins
and peanuts.

I'll end with french fries and pizza.

And, when I'm done,
I'll throw my napkin
away and…

I'll wipe my mouth
on my sleeve!

Chapter Three

Night Wish

I want to climb
the apple tree
outside my window.

I want to climb
the tree at night…

and get a piece of fruit…

and a piece of moon.

Then I will go to bed—
my pockets full—
one with fruit…

and the other
with moon.